Somewhere

Barbara K. Caravona

This is a work of fiction. All of the characters, names, incidents, organizations, and dialogue in this novel are either the products of the author's imagination or are used fictitiously.

Archway Publishing books may be ordered through booksellers or by contacting:

Archway Publishing
1663 Liberty Drive
Bloomington, IN 47403
www.archwaypublishing.com
1 (888) 242-5904

Interior Image Credit: Leo Price

ISBN: 978-1-4808-9509-6 (sc)
ISBN: 978-1-4808-9510-2 (hc)
ISBN: 978-1-4808-9508-9 (e)

Print information available on the last page.

Archway Publishing rev. date: 11/09/2020

Hi, I'm Myrtle and I want to go "Somewhere". I live in The Pink Hotel with my mom, Mimi. The only dachshund in the building, I am quite lovely with my wavy auburn coat. I always squirm and screech when Mimi brushes the tangles out of this coat. She reminds me I must suffer to be beautiful.

Sadly, right now, there is a pandemic everywhere, and I can't take my beauty anywhere. We must all stay home to escape the coronavirus. That big word reminds me of coronation, the night I was crowned "Queen of Canines" in The Pink Hotel. After all, I am a moxie doxie.

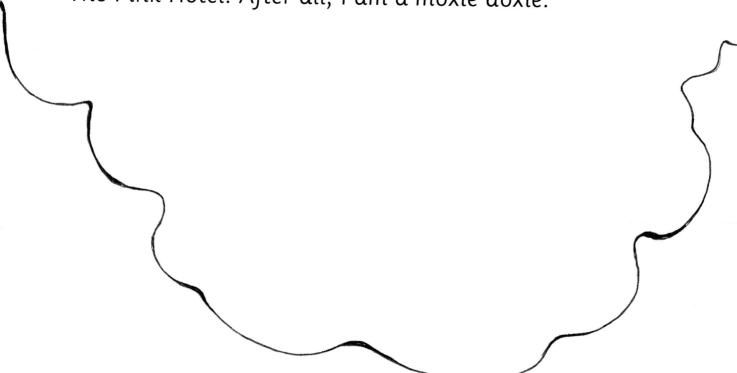

Anyway, I can't go Anywhere right now, and I want to go "Somewhere".

Shhh. I'm slipping into my pink dress and slipping out of The Pink Hotel. I better not bump into Dezi, my Bernese Mountain dog friend—she knows Mimi never lets me go Anywhere alone. Good thing Dezi and I see eye to eye.

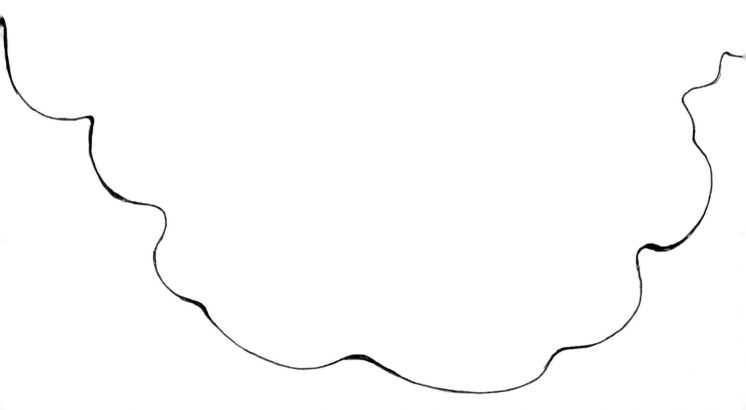

"Somewhere" ...

Whee!!!! First stop Niagara Falls, New York.
Dezi said it's a gigantic water park.

Whoa, I'm not leaping onto that water slide, so I buy a ticket for a boat ride under the Falls. Racing past a "Hot Dogs for Sale" sign, I snap up my size small yellow slicker (Dezi is an x-tra large!) and scurry aboard the "Maid of the Mist".

... wet, smiley

Next "Somewhere" ...

I've heard the longest cave in the whole world is in Kentucky at Mammoth Cave National Park. Wonder if they will let …. I'm in—dark, quiet, spooky. Lots of awesome bumps poke from the walls and ceiling inside the cave— oops, I trip over one. Round and round I go spilling out onto a ray of sunshine. Whew, very mammoth for this doxie but maybe just right for Dezi.

... shaky

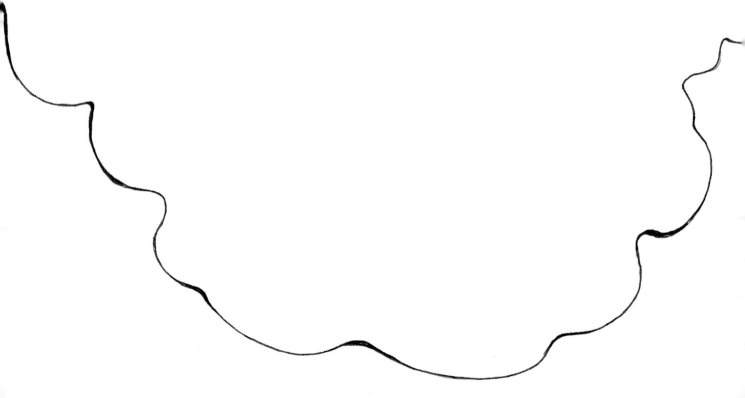

"Somewhere" different ...

Is Snake River in Idaho a river or a snake? I take a peek from Snake River Canyon and see both! Rattlesnakes slink smoothly along the banks of the winding blue-green river. I tiptoe away.

... silent

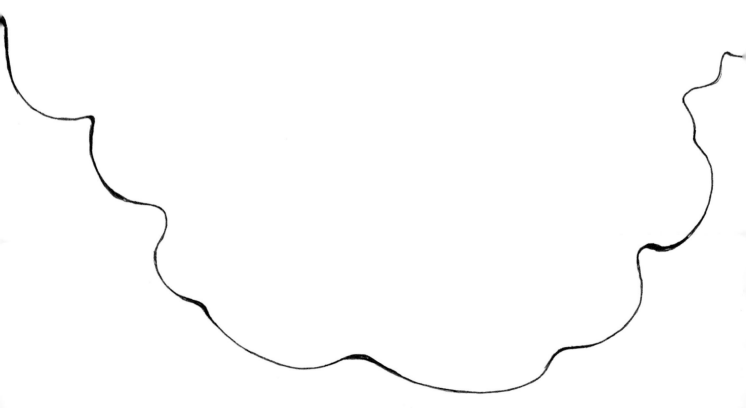

"Somewhere" else quickly …

Lonely for my faithful old Mimi, I decide to visit the "Old Faithful" geyser in nearby Wyoming. Swaddled in a beach towel, I eagerly lift my paw to dip into this famous fountain. Oh my!!!! Right in front of me, it spouts 350 degree steaming water 185 feet into the air. That's 185 doxies piled atop each other and 270 degrees hotter than the The Pink Hotel's swimming pool. No wading today for this moxie.

… lonely

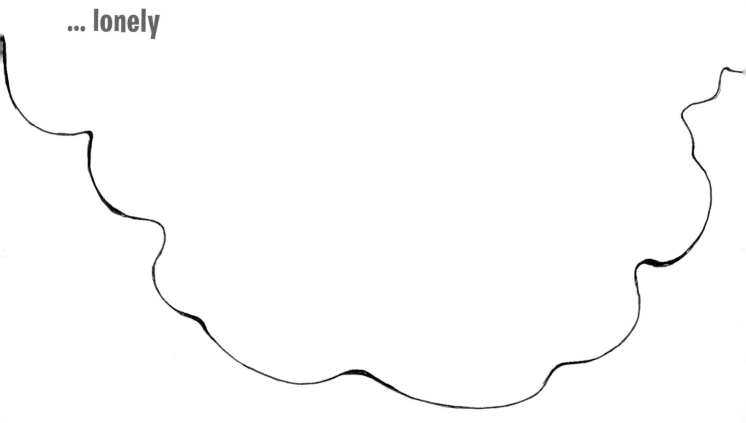

Last "Somewhere"

My final stop, Albuquerque (Al-boo-ker-key), New Mexico's hot-air balloon festival, is sure to lift my spirits. I jump into the basket barely in time for take-off (Dezi would burst the balloon!). Feeling blue away from The Pink Hotel, I've learned that being a guest "Somewhere" is good, but being home is better. With ears akimbo and heart thumping wildly, I soar to the sky.

... **hopeful**

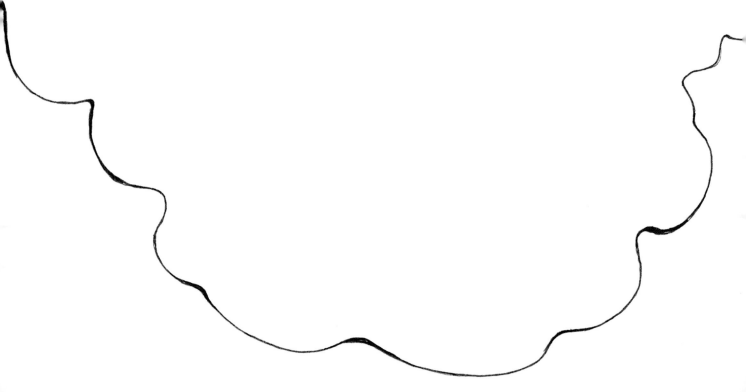

Birds turn colors flying through rainbows, and white clouds rest gently on green velvet treetops. Lake Erie, the warmest of the Great Lakes, comes into view and warms my doxie heart. Oh, there's Put-in-Bay, the island where sailors used to "put" themselves for protection from a choppy Lake Erie. It's time to "put" a doxie back to the shelter of The Pink Hotel.

... relieved

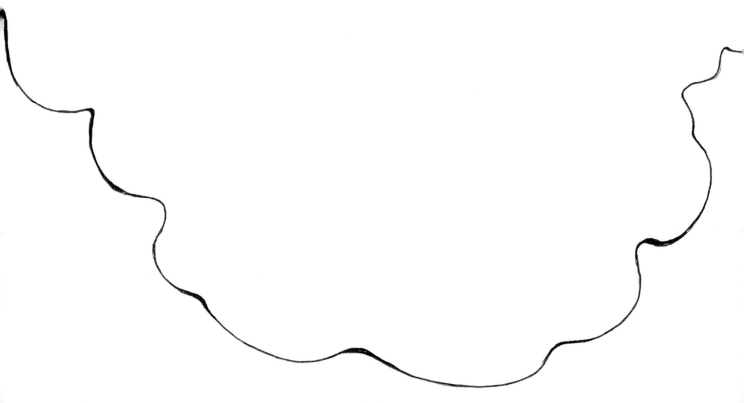

Favorite "Somewhere"

Rolled into a donut on my cushy bed, I hear a click open the door. Whoopie, it's Mimi! She kneels down to greet me. Fitting perfectly into her hug, I whisper, "Mimi, today I went "Somewhere."

... comfortable

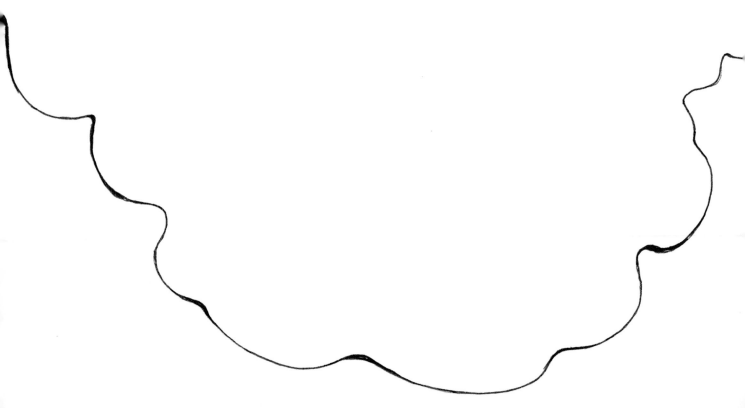

Last word —

When the uninvited guest, Coronavirus, fades away, Dezi and I will go Anywhere and Everywhere or just stay eye to eye at The Pink Hotel.

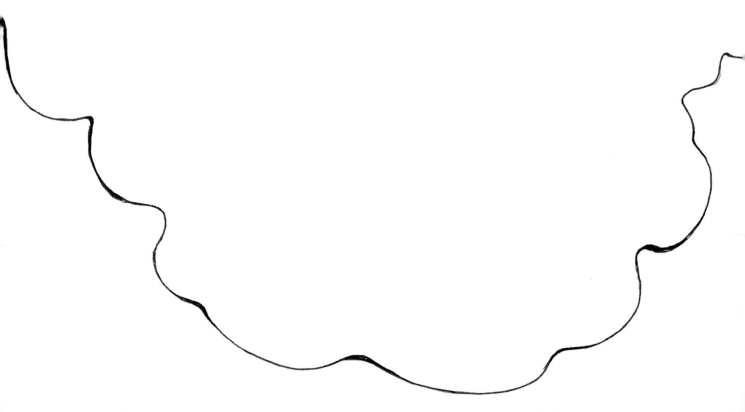

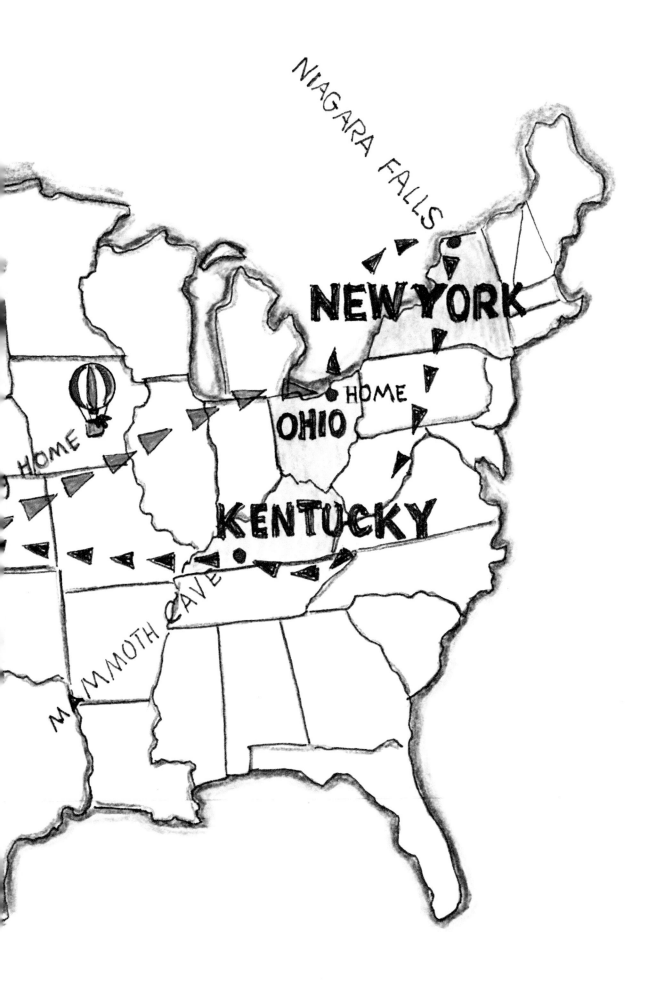

NIAGARA FALLS

NEW YORK

HOME

OHIO

KENTUCKY

MAMMOTH CAVE

HOME